A WOODLAND MYSTERY™

The Missing Will

A WOODLAND MYSTERY
By Irene Schultz

To Dr. Gene Cramer, who gave young people
the joy of reading

The Missing Will
©2000 Wright Group Publishing, Inc.
Text by Irene Schultz
Cover illustration by Meg Aubrey
Cameo illustrations by Taylor Bruce
Interior illustrations by Tom Sperling and Adam Weiskind

Woodland Mysteries™
© Wright Group Publishing, Inc.

The Wright Group
19201 120th Avenue NE
Bothell, WA 98011
www.WrightGroup.com

Printed in the United States of America

10 9 8 7 6 5 4 3 2 1

ISBN: 0-322-01956-7
ISBN: 0-322-02369-6 (6-pack)

What family solves mysteries ... has adventures all over the world ... and loves oatmeal cookies?

It's the Woodlanders!

Sammy Westburg (10 years old)
His sister Kathy Westburg (13)
His brother Bill Westburg (14)
His best friend Dave Briggs (16)
His best grown-up friend Mrs. Tandy
And Mop, their little dog!

The children all lost their parents, but with Mrs. Tandy have made their own family.

Why are they called the Woodlanders? Because they live in a big house in the Bluff Lake woods. On Woodland Street!

Together they find fun, mystery, and adventure. What are they up to now?

Read on!

Meet the Woodlanders!

Sammy Westburg
Sammy is a ten-year-old wonder!
He's big for his fifth-grade class, and
big-mouthed, too. He has wild hair
and makes awful spider faces. Even
so, you can't help liking him.

Bill Westburg
Bill, fourteen, is friendly and strong,
and only one inch taller than his
brother Sammy. He loves Sammy,
but pokes him to make him be
quiet! He's in junior high.

Kathy Westburg
Kathy, thirteen, is small, shy, and
smart. She wants to be a doctor
some day! She loves to be with
Dave, and her brothers kid her
about it. She's in junior high, too.

Dave Briggs

Dave, sixteen, is tall and blond. He can't walk, so he uses a wheelchair and drives a special car. He likes coaching high-school sports, solving mysteries, and reading. And Kathy!

Mrs. Tandy

Sometimes the kids call her Mrs. T. She's Becky Tandy, their tall, thin, caring friend. She's always ready for a new adventure, and for making cookies!

Mop

Mop is the family's little tan dog. Sometimes they have to leave him behind with friends. But he'd much rather be running after Sammy.

Table of Contents

Chapter 1:
The Woman with
the Crocodile Smile

One hot Saturday morning, four children
and a woman stood looking into the window of a shop in Green Forest. They were
from the next town, Bluff Lake. They lived

together in a house in the woods. They called themselves the Woodlanders.

The four children were orphans. The woman was their friend and helper, Mrs. Tandy.

The window was full of old things ...

a rusty gun

a lace dress

a wheel from a farm cart

a hunting knife

... and something else.

"Wow, look at that iron thing," said ten-year-old Sammy, pointing. He was big for his age, almost as big as his fourteen-year-old brother Bill. "What is it? It looks like a car part."

He scratched his head to show how hard he was thinking, and his wild hair got even wilder.

His sister, Kathy Westburg, who was thirteen, laughed and said, "This antique

shop sells a lot of things, but I don't think it sells car parts."

Sammy said, "Well, if YOU know so much, Kathy, tell me what that thing is."

Mrs. Tandy smiled and said, "I know what it's for, Sammy. It's for getting a pit out of a cherry. I could use that old cherry pitter if it still works."

Dave Briggs, sixteen, rolled his wheelchair in for a closer look. He said, "Let's go in and find out how much it costs."

Kathy said, "Oh, good idea. I love to look at antiques, but I hate to go in alone."

Dave pushed himself inside. The rest of the Woodlanders followed him.

Fourteen-year-old Bill walked in last. He was short for his age but very strong. He closed the door behind him.

A short, skinny woman hurried over to them. She smiled a fake smile and said, "I am sorry, but I don't have anything for children here. Why don't you wait outside?"

Dave looked her right in the eye and said, "We want to stay. We have very grown-up taste."

Mrs. Tandy said, "We will all stay. These children are my best friends."

Sammy added, "Don't worry. We won't break anything."

The shop owner's eyes looked mean

above her fake smile. But Bill asked anyway, "How much is that cherry pitter in the window?"

The shop owner said, "It costs too much for you. Everything in this store is VERY costly. Everything is far too costly for you children."

Mrs. Tandy spoke up. "Then I'd like to know."

She picked the cherry pitter up, but there was no price tag on it.

All of a sudden, there was an awful crash.

The store owner ran to the back room. They heard her talking in a low, mean voice.

"Hey," whispered Sammy, "why is she trying to get rid of us? She has the most fake smile, like a crocodile."

Dave said, "Maybe she thinks someone in a wheelchair is bad for her store."

5

Bill said, "Maybe she wants me to get out because I have brown skin."

Kathy joked, "Maybe she hates the braces on my teeth!" And they all laughed.

The shop owner came back, but now she talked in a sweet and friendly voice. She said, "Children, hurry. Come with me. Something fell over. Could you help my husband pick it up?"

Kathy, Bill, Dave, and Sammy looked hard at each other, but they and Mrs. Tandy followed her.

In the back room, a huge desk lay on its back. It was tall and had a large, smooth board across its front. The board covered some of the upper drawers. A key was stuck in the lock at the top of the board.

The children helped the man lift the desk back onto its feet.

Sammy said, "Boy, is this desk strong! That crash didn't hurt it at all."

The man said, "That's because it was so well made, in the time before the American Revolution, and ..."

"Jake Rut," the shop owner snapped, "keep your mouth shut!"

Dave asked, "How did it fall?"

The man said, "I guess I pushed a little too hard when I was trying to unlock the desk."

The woman snapped, "Never mind that!" She showed the children out of the back room.

Then she walked fast to the front of the shop. She got the cherry pitter from the window and pushed it into Mrs. Tandy's hands. "This is to pay for the children's work."

Then she went over to the door and held it open. "You'll have to leave now. I'm closing for the day."

Sammy pointed at the door. He said, "Gee, that's funny. That sign says, LIZA RUT—ANTIQUES. OPEN DAILY 9:00 TO 5:30. Funny that you're closing early Saturday morning."

Just then the strong, kind police chief from Bluff Lake walked in.

He said, "Hello, Becky. Hi, kids. I saw you through the window. I haven't seen you Woodlanders all week."

Sammy asked, "Hey, what are YOU doing in Green Forest? You belong to us in Bluff Lake."

Chief Hemster laughed. "Green Forest's police chief is away for a week. I'm watching over both towns. Now why don't we look around here together?"

Bill said, "We can't. Mrs. Rut here just told us she's closing."

Mrs. Rut smiled her widest crocodile smile. "Don't be silly, darling," she said. "I can't shut my store on six good customers, can I?"

"But you said ..." Sammy began.

"Don't worry, dear," Mrs. Rut broke in. "Just make yourselves at home. Take your time. Call me if you want to ask about anything."

She moved fast as a little lizard across the shop and into the back room.

Sammy whispered, "She's coo-coo! I've made up a great poem about her:

Mrs. Rut

Is a nut!"

Mrs. Tandy whispered, "My, I think you may be right, Sammy. Something is strange here." Quietly she told Chief Hemster how hard Mrs. Rut had tried to get rid of them.

The chief whispered, "It sounds almost like she's hiding something, doesn't it? Let's have that look around."

They spent a happy half–hour looking through the shop. They saw ...

a set of books made in 1850

a wolf trap
a steel dagger
an old lock with its key stuck
a tin washtub of big old keys
a hundred-year-old doll
a glass toothpick holder shaped like
a dog
… and a skinny little stuffed alligator.

Sammy held it up and whispered, "Hey, here's Mrs. Rut! It has her smile!"

Dave whispered, "That's an alligator. You said she smiled like a crocodile!"

Sammy said, "Well, she's both. She's a CROCO-GATOR."

The chief looked at his watch and whispered, "Let's get going. I'll treat you to ice cream and tell you a story about this place that you won't believe!"

Mrs. Tandy answered, "Sounds like a great plan." Then she called loudly, "Good-bye, Mrs. Rut."

11

Mrs. Rut came out of the back wearing her fake smile.

"Come back soon," she said. "It was so nice to meet you! And you children are so good."

They went out, and Sammy made his best poison-spider face. "So good?" he said. "She's so mean that ANYONE seems good next to her!"

Chapter 2:
The Missing Will

At the ice cream shop, Kathy chose a blueberry cone.

Sammy had to taste three new kinds. He ended up with good old chocolate mint.

Bill picked strawberry.

Dave took chocolate fudge.

Mrs. Tandy and Chief Hemster both got butter pecan.

They all began to walk to the park. Chief Hemster said, "Becky, we may be a perfect pair. I never knew you liked butter pecan."

Mrs. Tandy said, "Take me out for ice cream more often, John, and you'll find out a lot about me."

Sammy began dancing around and singing, "Mrs. Tandy's got a BOYfriend! Mrs. Tandy's got a BOYfriend!"

A sharp poke from Bill stopped him.

By the time Sammy caught up to Bill to poke him back, his ice cream was running down his elbow.

Bill and Kathy had to rinse him off in the drinking fountain.

Then they asked the chief to tell them

14

about Mrs. Rut's shop.

Here's what he said:

"Maybe you did not notice, but the shop is the first floor of a big old stone house.

"The walls are all made of stone and about four feet thick.

"It was the only house for miles around back in 1850.

"Some folks say it was built to hide run away slaves."

Dave asked, "Did the house always have stores around it? Or did they move the house downtown on rollers? I've read about how old houses are moved that way."

The chief said, "No, the house was always where it is now. The stores were built later, near the house."

Kathy asked, "Does someone still live on the floors above the shop?"

He answered, "Mr. and Mrs. Rut live there now.

"Until last year, Mrs. Morton, the eighty-nine-year-old woman who owned the house, lived there. She let her niece, Mrs. Rut, move in about ten years ago.

"Last year, Mrs. Morton died on a trip to visit a friend in New York. Mrs. Rut was her only living relative."

The chief lifted his hand. "Here's the

strange part. Mrs. Morton told her friend she had grown to hate her niece."

Bill said, "Boy, that's easy to understand."

Chief Hemster added, "Mrs. Morton told her friend she had left a will giving her furniture and other things to museums all over the country. She wanted her antiques to go to places like the White House. Or to Washington's house. Or to Thomas Jefferson's house.

"Mrs. Morton's husband was related to both Washington and Jefferson. Her friend said that some of the furniture came from Washington's and Jefferson's friends and families.

"Mrs. Morton knew the history of every piece of furniture. Her friend said that Mrs. Morton wrote the histories down.

"Those histories are very important to our country. If we could find them, they might make the furniture worth a lot more. Maybe even hundreds of thousands of dollars more."

Kathy said, "It must be hard for Mrs. Rut to give all of that up."

"That's just the trouble," said the chief. "She isn't giving it up. She says her aunt gave everything to HER. She even has a ten-year-old will to prove it, and a later will was never found. Nor was the history. Nor any money."

Dave asked, "Then nothing will go to the museums?"

The chief said, "No, Mrs. Rut and her husband will get everything."

The Woodlanders and Chief Hemster reached the park swings. Dave pushed Sammy. Back and forth he went.

Every time Sammy swung back he called out a few words to Dave.

"What if Mrs. Morton's friend was ...

"right, and Mrs. Morton wrote a new ...

"will! If I were a sneaky niece, I'd look all over ...

"and find that will, and I'd burn it!

"And if there were a written history of the furniture, I'd ...

"hide it. But if I were Mrs. Morton, I'd have ...

"made more than one copy because I'd know ...

"what a crocodile-sneak my niece Liza really was!"

By then, Dave was laughing. "Boy, you really think she's low! I guess Rut is a good name for her. You know how low a rut in a road can get."

Then Bill called, "Yes, and Liza is short for lizard, like a crocodile, but smaller and faster ... WATCH OUT, SAMMY!"

Sammy had jumped off the moving swing. He landed on his feet but had to keep running. He fell forward into a big sand pile and rolled over a few times. Finally, he jumped up.

"I did it!" he shouted.

Bill jumped off his swing and ran to him. "You OK, Sammy?"

Sammy said, "Sure. I've seen you do that for so long, I wanted to try."

Bill said, "But Sammy, I SLOW DOWN before I jump."

Sammy bragged, "Well, I might get into a book of world records for jumping!"

Mrs. Tandy said, "It's a good thing Kathy plans to be a doctor ... and the sooner the better."

Chief Hemster laughed and brushed the sand out of Sammy's hair. "What Sammy was saying is pretty much what some of my fellow police officers think. We are afraid the Ruts will end up cheating our country out of things that can never be replaced.

"But we searched carefully! We never found a new will. If we could ... I'd finally have a case against Mrs. Rut and her husband."

Dave said, "Looks to me as if the desk we picked up for her was a piece of Mrs. Morton's furniture ... and they're trying to open it."

Mrs. Tandy said, "Looks to me as if Mrs. Rut didn't want anyone to find out too much about it."

21

Sammy said, "Looks to me as if a family of super-snoopers might find some new clues in her shop."

Kathy said, "Looks to me as if she'd get mad if we went in there too often."

Chief Hemster said, "Looks to me as if someone who WORKED there might help us a lot."

Bill said, "Then it looks to me as if I need an after-school job. In an ANTIQUE shop. And in a hurry!"

Chapter 3:
Bill Gets a Job

The rest of the weekend, the whole
Woodland family was busy ... trying to
figure out a way to help Bill get a job
with Mrs. Rut. Even Mop, their shaggy

little tan dog, hung around.

Mrs. Tandy said, "The trouble is, if you just walk in and ask her, she might say 'no' and that will end that!"

Kathy said, "Maybe you can show her she needs you, before you ask her."

Sammy said, "How about if I go in with an ice cream cone? SPLAT! I'll drop it."

Dave asked, "What good will THAT do?"

Sammy said, "Then Bill will happen to walk in with a rag and pail and clean it right up."

Everyone laughed. Dave said, "I think she might suspect something."

At last, they all agreed, Bill would have to think of something himself.

Bill said, "That's all right. Monday I'll go in and do it! I'll get a job at her antique shop someway."

But inside, he was worried.

After school Monday, Bill rode his bike the two miles to Green Forest at double speed ... even though it was a very hot day.

He rode to the alley behind the shop. He saw a low window with iron bars on it. He locked his bike to the bars. Then he walked to the front door.

But a sign on it read:

```
SHOP CLOSED

OPEN AT 4:15 P.M.
```

He heard a woman's voice shouting from deep inside the shop. She sounded angry, but Bill couldn't hear her words clearly.

Bill decided, "I think I'll get my bike and ride around until four-fifteen."

So he walked back to the window where his bike was. He leaned over to unlock the chain. Suddenly, he found that he could hear every word from the back room!

"I'm telling you, Jake, we don't dare let the desk go yet. We have to check every last bit of it," the woman was saying.

"Another copy of the new will might be hidden in it," she went on. "I HAVE to make sure ... and burn it like I did the other copy. We've GOT to find the desk key!"

A man's voice shouted back, "Well, if you hadn't been so mean to your aunt, we wouldn't be in this fix! She'd have given these things to you."

"Be quiet, Jake!" the woman shouted.

"Just keep trying those keys.

"You've only tried about a tenth of them. ONE of them has to fit, but only my aunt knew which one. Try EVERY one of them, every way you can!"

Mr. Rut yelled, "If you are so smart, why did you wait to help me?"

She answered, "I kept thinking you'd be able to find it yourself. And I HAD to keep the shop going. We need all the money we can get."

She added, "Besides, the police might suspect us again if we close the shop without a reason. I wish we DID have a good reason to close for a few days. Then someone with BRAINS, like me, could find that key."

Mr. Rut shouted, "BRAINS! You're the one who told Mrs. Jackson she could buy the desk on Saturday. That's just five days away!"

Liza Rut yelled, "Well, I'm not going to let a fortune slip away! I'm getting that money on Saturday! You keep trying those keys!"

And she slammed out the front door.

Bill ran out of the alley.

"Wow, Chief Hemster was right!" he said to himself. "I heard their whole plan! But I don't have any proof at all." He smiled. "Just the same, I think I know how to get that job!"

He walked across the street thinking and working out his idea.

At 4:15 he saw Liza Rut return and unlock her door. A few minutes later Bill crossed the street and looked in. Mrs. Rut was standing on a ladder. She was holding a heavy mirror. She was trying to pull it up off the floor.

The ladder shook a little. She let go of the mirror and held on to the ladder with both hands.

Bill stepped into the shop. "Do you need some help, Mrs. Rut? I'll do that for you."

She said, "What are YOU doing here? You're one of the kids who were here the other day!"

Bill made himself speak out in a cheery voice. He said, "If you'll get off the ladder, I'll hang that mirror."

She said, "Wel-l-l, I guess I could use some help."

She stepped down. "But be careful with it," she said.

Bill climbed up. He said, "Sure. Give it to me."

Carefully he climbed up the ladder and hung the mirror. "Do you have anything else you want to hang on these other nails?"

She handed him two framed pictures. "Hang one on each side."

Bill hung the pictures where he was told.

"Now," he said, "how about some of these other walls?" She had him put up two more pictures.

Then she said, "That's all. Look around and see if there is some little thing you want for pay."

Bill said, "I don't need to look around to know what I want. I want an after-school job!"

He gulped hard as he said it. He always felt afraid people would say "no" when he asked for a job.

Mrs. Rut smiled her crocodile smile and said, "No. I don't want a kid hanging around breaking things."

Bill said, "I don't break things, I FIX them. I can repair things and paint walls. But of course, if you had me paint, you'd have to close your shop for a few days. I guess you wouldn't want to do that."

Liza Rut gasped. She said, "Wait a minute! I'd have to close the shop for a few days?" Then she smiled her sly smile. "What's your name?"

"Bill," he said.

"You're hired, Bill! Make a sign, CLOSED FOR REPAIRS. Stay out of the back room. Don't talk to my husband, and don't waste any time.

"Lock the shop right now and start hanging these iron tools on that wall. But get that CLOSED sign up first."

An hour later it was 5:30. Mrs. Rut came out of the back room and handed Bill some money.

She said, "Don't come back tomorrow."

Bill's heart sank. He asked himself, "What did I do wrong? Why has she fired me already?"

But then she added, "We will be out

of town tomorrow. Come back Wednesday, right after school."

He thanked her and left quietly. But after he walked around the corner he was out of her sight. He jumped into the air. He threw out his arms like a football player after a touchdown. He did a happy little dance.

When he got to his bike and leaned down to unlock it, he got another earful from the window.

"Say, Jake!" he heard Liza Rut say. "You just put that key back in the crock! Haven't you been putting them into this tub after you try them, like I told you to?"

"Um, yes, yes!" Jake answered. "Um, that one was just a mistake."

"Well," she said, "the pile in the crock looks nearly as high as it did when you started. I wonder how many mistakes you've made!

"It's lucky for you that kid showed up! Now I'll be able to check the keys myself for the next few days ... and get it done RIGHT!"

Chapter 4:
Getting Ready for Trouble

The whole Woodland family and Chief Hemster were waiting for Bill when he got home. They ran down the front steps to meet him.

"Did you do it?" Kathy asked.

"Did you get the job?" Sammy yelled.

"Yep!" Bill said. "I got it!"

Sammy clapped and shouted, "Wow!" He went to the steps and poured a glass of ice water for Bill to drink.

Bill bowed. Then he told them about how he got the job. And he told them everything he remembered.

Dave said, "Boy, are you brave!"

Sammy slapped Bill so hard on the back, he made the ice water splash.

Bill said, "Cut that out, Sammy." But Sammy just did it again anyway.

So Bill splashed some ice water onto Sammy.

Sammy jumped up. He shouted, "Did everyone see that? Did you see what Bill did for no reason at all? And after I gave him the idea to get a job with Liza Rut?"

"Oh, come on, Sammy!" Bill said.

36

The next second they were both rolling on the ground, grunting like little baby bears.

Kathy quietly got up. She picked up the pitcher of ice water and handed it to Dave.

Dave reached over above the two boys and turned the pitcher upside-down.

The next thing Bill and Sammy knew they were both soaked with ice water.

They got up like mad, wet roosters and shook themselfves.

Kathy let out a giggle.

Then Bill saw how funny Sammy looked. His hair was as wild as an old toothbrush. Bill laughed out loud.

Then Bill opened his belt and pulled out his shirt. An ice cube fell out of the front.

Sammy began to giggle, too.

Then Mrs. Tandy said, "Since we're all here acting like a bunch of nuts, we might as well eat our nutty dessert before dinner. She went in and came out with nut-covered taffy apples.

Sammy led the others in wild clapping and shouts of "hurrah!"

■   ■   ■

Later, when they went inside, Mrs. Tandy said, "We have a lot to talk over,

Bill. None of us likes the idea of your being at the Ruts' alone."

They washed and sat down to one of their favorite meals ...

hamburgers with lettuce and tomatoes

raw string beans, sweet and crunchy

... and fruit cut up into little pieces, soaked in orange juice.

Mrs. Tandy said, "I'm thankful for this good food."

Sammy was starving. "Boy, I'm hungry as a wolf," he said. But he said it so fast, it sounded like it was one big word. "I'm h u n g r y a s a w o l f!"

He opened his mouth and half a hamburger went down in one bite. He grinned and said, "Now let's talk about our plans."

Dave looked at Bill. He said, "Well, Bill, here's what we've all been thinking so far. Wednesday after school, I'll drive you to Green Forest.   I'll park near the shop."

Sammy said, "We'll all be somewhere near it."

Kathy said, "With so much money at risk, Mrs. Rut might be a real danger."

Sammy said, "She might act up, like some dumb brothers do ... just because of a little bit of spilled water."

Mrs. Tandy said, "I think it won't look too odd if Kathy and I walk by, do you? We can do it a few times. Then you can signal if you need help."

Bill said, "That would look OK.   When a kid starts a new job, sometimes his family hangs around."

Dave asked, "Why don't you take one of our cell phones?"

Bill said, "Sure, I can put it in my backpack.   But aren't you all a little bit TOO worried?"

Chief Hemster said, "Some people go crazy over money. I think Liza Rut is that kind of person."

Sammy said, "Here's what I'm going to do. I'll ride my bike to Green Forest after school. I'll lock it up on those window bars and sit and do homework."

Sammy added, "If anyone comes out and sees me, I'll say I'm just waiting for Bill. Meanwhile, I'll listen."

"Good idea," said Dave.

The chief said, "I can't tell you what a big step ahead this is. I asked the F.B.I. to have an agent trail the Ruts tomorrow, ... because Bill found out they were going out of town. If you Woodlanders can crack this case, the F.B.I. will want to be in on it."

After dinner Bill said, "Oh, I forgot to tell you about one thing. You know, Mrs. Rut is really mad about not finding that desk key. She yells at her husband Jake for everything.

"Today she was mad because he put a key back in a crock. Only the un-tried keys are supposed to be in the crock. The ones he has tried are supposed to go into a tub."

The chief said, "If only we could come up with a way to keep the Ruts from finding the right key before they sell the desk."

Sammy asked, "What good would THAT do?"

The chief answered, "They might become more greedy. They might sell the desk without opening it."

Bill said, "I see. And we can search it later for a copy of the will. Then Mrs. Morton's antiques would go to a museum, where they belong."

As Bill said this, an idea flashed into his mind.

He said, "I know how to keep the Ruts from finding that desk key before Saturday! Sammy, do you still have the tape we made for Halloween? You remember ... one with the dogs barking and all the other noises?"

The other Woodlanders and Chief Hemster listened as Bill told his plan.

Then the chief said, "I'll be in Green Forest tomorrow afternoon, too. If you need me, Dave can reach me on his car phone. Good luck tomorrow!"

And off he went.

■   ■   ■

After school Tuesday, the Woodlanders got ready. They charged the batteries in their cell phones. They put the tape into the small tape player. They checked over Sammy's bike.

Dave had taken out some library books. The books were all about furniture from the early days of America ... before the United States was even a country.

Mrs. Tandy said, "Let's see what the furniture from George Washington's time looked like. Let's see if we can find one like the desk that fell."

They turned the pages until all of a sudden Kathy pointed at one, and gasped,

44

"Hey, isn't that almost like the one at Mrs. Rut's store?"

In front of their eyes was a picture marked FALL FRONT DESK. 1690–1720.

Bill said, "You're right! I remember those big sort-of-flat balls on the bottoms of the legs. It says here that's rare."

Kathy said, "And I remember that thick molding at the top. I remember thinking no wonder it fell over. It looks so top-heavy."

Sammy joked, "I think this book made a mistake. They call it a 'Fall Front Desk,' but the one we lifted up fell BACK!"

Dave said, "Come on, Sammy! They mean that big front board that covers the upper drawers. That front board swings down to write on when you open the desk."

Mrs. Tandy said, "This one was made more than seventy-five years before the Revolutionary War.

"That desk in the Ruts' back room really could have belonged to George Washington."

Bill said, "Boy, we'd have fun looking inside of a desk like that. This one in the book has more than forty little drawers and secret hiding places."

Dave said, "Well, we'd better get to our homework … so we're ready for tomorrow. Good night, everyone."

"Good night," Kathy said.

"Good night," Mrs. Tandy said.

"Good night, Ice Cube Belly," Sammy called to Bill. Then he ran to his room.

Chapter 5:
The Great Idea

It was Wednesday after school at last.

Dave was in his van, just down the street from the antique shop.

Sammy was at the shop's back window.

Kathy and Mrs. Tandy were down at the library.

Bill was in Mrs. Rut's shop.

Mrs. Rut said, "I've decided to get you started painting the walls. I need to work with my husband in the back room.

"Lock the door."

Bill asked, "Do you have the paints and brushes and rollers and ..."

She said, "Yes, yes, everything is there in the corner.

"Just see that no one bothers me."

She went into the back room and closed the door.

Bill started painting near that door.

As he moved the furniture away from the walls he listened. But he couldn't hear the Ruts.

He shouted through the back room door. "Mrs. Rut, I'm going out for a few minutes.

"I'll take the front door key to let myself back in."

He grabbed the phone from his back pack.

The minute he was away from the shop, he called Dave.

He said, "Dave, now's the time to stop the Ruts! Get Sammy and meet me at the corner."

Two minutes later, Bill and Sammy were in Dave's van.

Five minutes later Sammy was back in the alley. He had his phone. And he was carrying the tape recorder with the tape in it.

It was the tape he had made for Halloween night.

"Ready?" he said into the phone. "OK, here it goes, Bill!"

He set the tape recorder for LOUD. He slid it behind a dumpster.

Horrible noises went booming through the alley: SQUEALS! HOWLS! SHOUTS! SCREAMS!

Several shops besides the Ruts' had back doors into the alley.

The owners ran out of them to find out what was making the noise.

Finally, the Ruts ran out of THEIR alley door, too.

At that moment, Bill's cell phone rang, one ring from Sammy.

Bill raced into the front door of the shop.

He grabbed a big empty pail and ran into the back room.

He stopped in front of the big crock of keys ... dumped the keys into the empty pail ... and dumped the keys from the tub into the crock.

Then he dumped the keys from the pail into the tub.

He grabbed the empty pail and ran it to the front room.

He hurried out the front door and locked it.

He called Sammy's cell phone, let it ring once, and ran.

Outside in back, Mrs. Rut had caught sight of Sammy.

He was doing a wild dance in the middle of the alley. He was waving his arms. He was kicking his feet into the air.

Mrs. Rut ran over to him and screamed, "Where is that noise coming from? Did you start it? Well STOP it!"

Sammy didn't stop his wild dance ... until the cell phone in his pocket gave that one ring.

Then he ran over to the dumpster. He pulled out his tape recorder. He turned it off.

He made an angel face and said, "Oh, does my music bother you?"

Mrs. Rut made a fist and shook it in Sammy's face.

She screamed, "Do you call that MUSIC? Get out of my alley! If you ever come back, you'll be sorry!"

Bill came through the shop's front door again ... just as the Ruts came into the front room.

Mrs. Rut said, "Too bad for you, Bill. You missed a crazy boy in the alley.

"His hair was wild, and he was playing horrible music. Anyway, he called it music.

"Lucky for everyone I was there to get things under control."

She said it as if she had done something very important. She even grinned her crocodile smile.

Bill said, "Why doesn't something exciting happen when I'm around? Well, I'd better get on with painting."

An hour later, at five thirty, it was time for him to stop.

He said, "Goodbye, Mrs. Rut. Wish I'd had a chance to see that crazy kid."

And he headed off for home … where the crazy kid lived!

Chapter 6:
The Wednesday Night Reports

By dinnertime, two cars were parked in the driveway of the Woodland family's house.

One belonged to Chief Hemster.

The other belonged to Mr. Street, the F.B.I. agent.

The chief and Sammy got out of the police car. Chief Hemster was carrying a HUGE pail of fried chicken.

Sammy was carrying a bag full of mashed potatoes, slaw, and hot rolls. He was carrying one of the rolls in his mouth, chewing while he walked.

Mr. Street followed them.

Bill and Dave and Mrs. Tandy and Kathy were already there. Chief Hemster had them meet Mr. Street.

Mrs. Tandy said, "Go right to the dinner table. We have plates and coffee and milk out already."

They washed and sat down.

The chief said, "First, tell us about this key exchange. Sammy's been talking about it."

Mrs. Tandy said, "My, yes. Let's hear

the whole story, Bill.

"Right when we were going to visit the shop, we saw you shoot out the door, like a runaway puppy.

"Then you stopped to use your cell phone."

Dave said, "That was when he called me!"

Kathy said, "Sammy ran out of the alley and came back."

Mrs. Tandy said, "It was like watching a Marx Brothers film. Or some kind of crazy cartoon."

Kathy said, "You could have heard the noise for a mile. And Sammy was jumping up and down like a giant grasshopper."

Chief Hemster said to Mr. Street, "You see, we needed a way to draw the Ruts out the back door. Then Bill could switch the keys.

"He replaced the ones that might work on the desk with the ones that WOULDN'T work. That will stop the Ruts from opening the desk."

Sammy said, "I danced my brains out while Bill changed the keys.

"You might call me the 'key' man in the plan." He laughed at his own joke. "Hey, get it? KEY man."

Everyone groaned.

Bill said, "The Ruts talked about it for the rest of the day."

Sammy said, "Great! Well, I'm still the best detective. Wait until you hear what I found out!"

"What?" they asked.

But by then Sammy was munching on his fourth chicken leg.

Three huge bites later he said, "I was snooping at the back window before Bill called me. I heard Mrs. Rut tell her husband that they needed money fast. She's going to sell the only piece of furniture her aunt left her."

"No!" said Chief Hemster. "She hasn't wanted to sell any of the pieces."

Sammy went on. "She said that all her aunt had left her was a school desk, 'a crummy school desk,' she called it. So she's selling it.

"I saw it in the window, too. It's about Kathy's size."

Mrs. Tandy said, "Why did her aunt leave her anything? She'd KNOW Mrs. Rut would just sell it."

Dave said, "That's a good question. I think we should buy that desk. Think about it. Mrs. Morton must have known that Mrs. Rut would never be interested in it. It would be a perfect hiding place."

Mr. Street spoke up next. "I want to tell you about a trip I made yesterday.

You know I trailed the Ruts."

"Where did they go?" everyone asked.

"To New York and back," he said.

"My heavens, that's quite a day's trip," exclaimed Mrs. Tandy. "A few hundred miles each way."

Dave asked, "Why did they go? Did you find out?"

"Yes, indeed," Mr. Street answered. "They went to sign the final papers for the sale of the big desk, to an antique collector."

"Is he a crook?" Sammy asked.

"She," said Mr. Street. "And no, she's no crook. Her name is Mrs. Jackson. She works for a museum. I talked to her after they left. I told her everything.

"She will help us Saturday. She's going to use marked money the F.B.I. loaned her to buy the desk. That way we can prove the Ruts sold it to her."

"Does she know about our search for the will?" Bill asked.

"Yes," said Mr. Street. "And she is eager to help us solve this case."

"Meanwhile," Chief Hemster said, "I agree with Dave. I think we must buy that school desk. And I think Becky Tandy is the one to do it."

Mr. Street asked, "How can Mrs. Tandy do that without making the Ruts think she knows something?"

Kathy said, "And how can you even get Mrs. Rut to open the shop? It still says CLOSED FOR REPAIRS."

Chief Hemster said, "Don't worry. If anyone can do it, Becky can."

Mrs. Tandy said, "I think I have an idea. And tomorrow, Kathy, I think you'll own a desk. Happy birthday."

Kathy said, "But my birthday isn't for months, Mrs. Tandy."

"Well," said Mrs. Tandy with a smile, "I like to do my shopping early."

Chapter 7:
The Little School Desk

The next morning everyone got up early for breakfast.

"Hey!" Sammy said to Mrs. Tandy. "You look really extra sharp this morning.

High heels. Your best suit. What's going on?"

She answered, "Well, Sammy, I found out years ago that if you want to impress someone in a hurry, you try to look very sharp. These are my open-the-door-Mrs.-Rut clothes."

"Good luck," laughed Dave. "You do look like you have money and might spend it. That's just the thing to impress Mrs. Rut."

As he was going out, Sammy called, "Mrs. Tandy, if you think you need me to protect you, pick me up at school. I'm sure my teacher can spare me for the morning."

Bill laughed. "Spare you for the morning?" he called. "I bet she can spare you for the whole month!

"After you left your huge hairy rubber spider under a paper on her desk!

"And she screamed so loud they heard her in the front office!

"And you had to write you'd never do it again, two hundred times!

"I bet she'd spare you for the whole school year!"

Sammy said, "I only put it there in case she wanted it for a science lesson."

Then he ran back in and poked Bill and ran to the door again.

Dave said, "OK, guys. No more teasing. Time to get to school."

And off they went.

■   ■   ■

Mrs. Tandy took her best purse. Then she drove to the Ruts' antique store.

She looked in the window at the little desk.

"Why that's the same kind I had in school," she was thinking. "That desk isn't more than forty years old! To be an antique, it should be at least one hundred. But the sign says ANTIQUE DESK. What a cheat!"

It was both a desk and seat, held together by a metal frame.

Below the seat was a deep, roomy drawer. In the desk top, at the front, was a hole for an old ink bottle to fit in.

"Well, here goes," Mrs. Tandy said to herself.

She knocked on the door ... Bang! Bang! Bang!

No answer.

She knocked again, louder ... BANG! BANG! BANG!

This time, a sour-faced Mrs. Rut stepped out of the back room. She shook her head no and pointed to the CLOSED sign.

BANG! BANG! BANG!

This time, a very angry-looking Mrs. Rut marched to the front door. She opened it and said, "Can't you read! We are closed for repairs!"

She began to slam the door shut when Mrs. Tandy said, "I won't take much time. I came to buy a gift.

"When I saw that dear desk in the window, and had the money right here, I felt I'd risk a knock on your door."

"Oh, you want to buy that desk! Well, why didn't you say so? It's priced very low and is in good shape. It's a hundred years old."

Mrs. Rut gave Mrs. Tandy her crocodile smile. "I can only accept cash."

Mrs. Tandy paid her, and soon she drove off with the desk.

■   ■   ■

After Bill worked Thursday afternoon, everyone met at the Woodlanders' home. Mr. Street and Chief Hemster went there, too.

Sammy had little to report from listening at the back window. "She just kept saying things like, 'Oh, turn it harder,' and 'YOU must have missed the right key!'

"If I were Jake, I'd feel like putting a key in her mouth ... and locking it for keeps!"

Mrs. Tandy told them about shopping for the little desk.

Kathy asked, "Did she act as if she might suspect anything?"

Mrs. Tandy answered, "I don't think so. She was just glad to get rid of the desk."

The chief said, "Well, let's take a look at it."

They gathered around it. Mrs. Tandy said, "I've already looked in the drawer. See, all that's there is a gum wrapper."

Sammy said, "I see it. It's stuck on a wad of gum. I wonder what flavor it is."

Kathy said, "Look, it's just like a gum wrapper made now, with that little arrow on it."

They pulled out the drawer and searched the space it fit into.

They looked at the bottom of the desk.

They examined the outside of the drawer.

They found nothing.

"Rotten rats!" Sammy said at last. "I give up!"

"What's our next move?" Dave asked.

Mr. Street said, "To watch the Ruts like hawks and hope to catch them in some slip-up.

"We know they are lying ... but knowing is not the same as being able to prove it."

"No," said Dave. "U.S. laws are based on the idea that no one is guilty of a crime unless PROVED guilty."

"Well," said Sammy, "let's hope that by Saturday the Ruts prove THEMSELVES guilty."

Chapter 8:
The First Secret
Hiding Place

Friday after school, the Woodlanders took their places in Green Forest again.

But now Mrs. Tandy, Kathy, and Dave all sat in Dave's van. They had books all around them, about ten of them. The books all showed secret hiding places in old furniture.

"It was so nice of our librarian to get them for us from other libraries," Kathy said.

Dave said, "It's lucky for us that the libraries in our state have inter-library loans."

Kathy said, "Look at this picture, Dave. The whole top molding on this dresser is hollow."

Dave said, "How about this? In this desk, you take out the drawer and look into the hole. The wood at the back moves forward. It opens up a space as wide as the desk."

Mrs. Tandy said, "This book shows how to make a secret hiding place. Pry off the front part of a thick drawer. Drill a fat, deep hole at the very bottom of the drawer front.

"Put in a note. Nail the drawer back together."

"Look at this one," Dave said. "An extra-thick desktop is made of two sheets of wood. You take off the edge. Then lift up one of the sheets of wood. And in between are secret papers!"

"Wow!" said Mrs. Tandy. "There must be a thousand ways to make a secret hiding place."

Kathy said, "Look at these ball feet. One ball is hollow. Twist the ball, and it unscrews. There's a little hiding place in it."

Dave said, "How about this one! Take out the drawers. Press a button. The inside back comes out."

Kathy said, "Oh Dave, do you think the F.B.I. agents will ever get a chance to look at the big desk?

"Do you think the Ruts will let Mrs. Jackson pick it up tomorrow?

"Do you think IT has any secret hiding places?

"Do you ..."

"Whoa, there, Kathy!" Dave said. "You look as bright as a chipmunk with a pile of nuts in front of her nose."

Kathy blushed. Secret hiding places had made her forget she was shy.

Dave said, "My guess is, the Ruts WILL sell the desk Saturday. They need money!"

Mrs. Tandy said, "I do hope Mr. Street will want our help. I want to search the desk for secret hiding places."

Dave said, "And I bet we could find one, too, because of reading all these books."

Mrs. Tandy said, "I feel as if I asked some experts and they told me how to do it.

"It's as if they were waiting in their books for us to come along to listen to them."

Kathy said, "Wait a minute! Someone DOES want us to listen. There's the car phone!"

It was Sammy calling. He said, "Come quick and pick up me and my bike. I'm at the corner two blocks north of the antique shop."

"We'll be right there, Sammy," Dave answered.

In two minutes they had Sammy's bike in the back of the van and Sammy in his seat. His face was dirty and his hair stuck out like a porcupine's quills.

Mrs. Tandy asked, "What's up, Sammy? Why are you so upset?"

Sammy said, "Here it is only half a day before Mrs. Jackson gets the desk ... and Liza Rut has spoiled EVERYTHING!"

"What's wrong?" Mrs. Tandy asked. "Oh my, is Bill all right?"

"Oh sure, it's nothing like that," Sammy said.

Kathy said, "Tell us, Sammy. I bet it's not so terrible."

"It's terrible!" Sammy said. "It's just awful! Mrs. Rut just made a phone call. It's horrible!"

Dave laughed, "Nothing can be so awful and horrible about a phone call."

"Oh yeah?" said Sammy. "Well, she called a LOCKSMITH! She told him she needs him to open a desk!"

"That's horrible!" said Dave.

"That's awful!" said Kathy.

"That's terrible!" said Mrs. Tandy.

"See!" said Sammy. "I told you so!"

■   ■   ■

When Bill got home at 5:30 Friday, he had no idea about the locksmith.

The rest of the family told him what Sammy had heard.

Sammy said, "I had to get out of the alley fast. What if the locksmith had come right over and the Ruts had found me there! I heard her tell him, 'It's an emergency!'"

Bill said, "I heard the back door slam right before I left. I bet he's there now."

They called Chief Hemster and told him

about the locksmith.

"Well," he said. "There's not a thing we can do about it. At least we kept her from opening that desk until tonight. We'll just have to wait and hope that she doesn't find a second copy of the will. I'll call Mr. Street."

Mrs. Tandy said, "Ask him to have dinner here with all of us. We have some books to show you."

After dinner, everyone looked at the books together.

All of a sudden Dave said, "Let's go over the little desk again.

"I feel sure Mrs. Morton left it to Mrs. Rut because she knew Mrs. Rut WOULD sell it. It HAS to have a message somewhere.

"She might even have made a secret

hiding place herself ... like the book showed."

Bill said, "Well, if you ask me, there's something funny about the gum wrapper in the drawer."

"What?" asked Mr. Street.

"It's too clean to be old," Bill answered. "There's no dust or dirt on it."

Mr. Street exclaimed, "You're right! It IS too clean!"

Dave said, "If I were going to leave a secret message, I'd use an arrow to point to it, maybe. Like the one on the gum wrapper. That arrow points ..."

"Under the drawer front!" everyone said at once.

In a minute, Bill had a hammer and had tapped the drawer front off. He turned it up-side down.

They felt their hearts pound! In the thick drawer-front's bottom, someone had

drilled a fat hole.   It ran up inside the
drawer front.

Inside was a white rolled-up piece of
paper.

Chapter 9:
The Will Is Found at Last

Kathy said, "I'll get some tweezers."

Mr. Street used them to pull the paper out. Rolled in the paper was another surprise. There were some strips of thin

All my things except a small school desk I leave to the United States of America, which I love so well.

This furniture has come to me from the friends and relatives of some of the most famous people in our history, George Washington and Thomas Jefferson.

Many of the items in my collection were used by people who fought for our country's freedom. These antiques have interest for museums.

I would like the furniture offered to these places:

1. Washington's home at Mount Vernon
2. Thomas Jefferson's home at Monticello
3. The White House

The small school desk goes to my niece, Lisa Rut.

My money should be used to help teach children about our past.

—Betty Morton

plastic with tiny rows of dots on them.

Here's what the paper said:

"All my things except a small school desk, I leave to the United States of America, which I love so well.

"This furniture has come from relatives of some of the most famous people in our history, George Washington and Thomas Jefferson.

"Many of the items in my collection were used by people who fought for our country's freedom. These antiques have interest for museums.

"I would like the furniture offered to these places:

1. Washington's home at Mount Vernon.

2. Thomas Jefferson's home at Monticello.

3. The White House.

"The small school desk goes to my niece, Liza Rut.

"My money should be used to help teach children about our past.

Betty Morton"

Dave said, "This paper is dated just five years ago! It's the newer will!"

Mr. Street looked at the will. He said, "I believe this will is legal."

At the end of the paper was this note:

"These plastic strips hold hundreds of pages of true stories about my furniture and papers. They explain why these items are so valuable."

Sammy pointed to the plastic strips. "That must be what they call microfilm. I bet every little dot is a whole page!"

Mr. Street said, "Right, Sammy. I can have a microfilm reading machine here by mid-morning tomorrow."

Mrs. Tandy said, "Now it won't matter what Mrs. Rut finds in the big desk. We have a will right here."

Kathy said, "But she tried to steal everything, and now she'll get away with that, won't she?"

"No," said Mr. Street. "About a minute after the sale of the desk ... Mrs. Rut will be under arrest."

Sammy grinned and said, "Too bad for Mrs. Rut. She should have kept her little desk and opened a little school for little crooks!"

■   ■   ■

The next morning they all met for breakfast in Green Forest. They had Mop with them in Dave's van.

"There's no telling what time we will get home again. This way we won't have to worry about Mop," said Mrs. Tandy.

They all waited for one sound. At last they heard it, the pager on Mr. Street's belt.

He said, "That's it. Mrs. Rut has taken money for something that wasn't hers.

"The truck has left the Morton house

with the big desk. It's now headed to an F.B.I. garage in Green Forest. Come on, Woodlanders! Let's see what the desk holds."

Kathy said, "I'm so excited! I hoped we'd be in on the hunt."

Mr. Street said, "You don't think Chief Hemster and I would search the desk alone, do you? You made yourselves into experts with those books. We need your help."

"Hurrah!" yelled Sammy as he jumped into the van. "Let me at that old desk!"

Chapter 10:
Forty-Two Secrets

They drove to the garage. An F.B.I agent
let them in. The desk stood in the
middle of the clean garage floor. Padded
covers like the ones on moving trucks lay

under and all around it. There were big folding tables set up, too.

Chief Hemster said, "Woodlanders, I'd like you to meet Mrs. Jackson, who bought the desk. She actually works for a museum. Mrs. Jackson, this is the Woodland family I've been telling you so much about."

They all shook hands.

Then Mrs. Jackson said, "I hate to start out with bad news, but I think the Ruts found a secret hiding place and took something from it. There's a false back behind a drawer. I found it jammed open a little bit and empty."

"Rotten rats!" said Sammy. "She's Mrs. RAT, not Mrs. Rut."

Dave said, "Don't give up so fast, Sammy. We can still look."

Sammy said, "But WE wanted to find the secret hiding place ... Hey, do you think there might be more than one?"

"One of the books showed a desk with forty," Kathy said.

Mr. Street said, "Let's try our luck."

Mrs. Jackson said, "About three of us can work standing in front of the desk. Then the other five can each work on a drawer."

Dave said, "Kathy and I can work on one of the big drawers."

Kathy blushed and said, "OK, Dave."

So Mrs. Jackson put a big drawer onto a table. She handed small ones to the others.

She said, "Before you begin, I must ask you to be very careful! If you find anything that looks like a hiding place, call me over and I will open it." Then she and Bill and Mrs. Tandy began looking over the desk.

Mrs. Jackson said, "Remember! Don't

bump anything, even a little bit. Each one of us may be holding a piece of our country's history. We don't want to chip it!"

Everyone began to look at a drawer.

After a while Dave said, "It seems to me we've pushed and pulled on every corner a hundred times."

Kathy said, "And pressed on the drawer handles, and tried to slide the sides up and down."

Dave said, "We've done everything except stand on our heads."

Sammy said, "Me, too. I'd hit it, if it weren't so old!"

Then he did turn it over and gently tapped its bottom. And SPANG! The bottom edge of the back opened up!

There was a hiding place! Inside the drawer back!

"YOW! Look at this!"

Everyone crowded around him. He said, "I knew there was a secret hiding place! It's a good thing I was here to find it."

He held the drawer on the table while Mrs. Jackson took two papers from the opening. One, a small one, said, "Desk 23."

Mrs. Jackson said, "We won't un-fold this big one now. A paper expert must do that. But here, Sammy. Look inside it, at the top, and then the bottom."

Sammy read out loud, "My dear husband," and from the bottom he read, "Love, Martha."

Mrs. Tandy cried, "Maybe this desk DID belong to George Washington! Maybe the Martha is Martha Washington!"

Mrs. Jackson said, "Mrs. Rut said the desk was Washington's!"

Chief Hemster said, "If Mrs. Rut told you the truth about that, it was the first time she has told the truth since this case began."

"WOW!" Sammy yelled. He pumped his fists up and down in the air. Then he ran around the whole garage. "The detective champ strikes again."

Bill said, "You mean the detective chimp. Now calm down before you break something."

"Let's keep looking," Sammy said, "Give me another drawer."

Mrs. Jackson said, "I'll put the things we find into folders, to be looked at later. The museum experts have a way to open papers without breaking them.

"See, I'll mark on the folder which drawer it came from. And I'll add a paper telling how to open the drawer."

Dave asked, "What do you think the twenty-three means?"

Mrs. Jackson said, "What do you think, Dave?"

Dave said, "Can it be there are at least twenty-two other hiding places in the desk? Did Sammy just happen to find the twenty-third?"

Mrs. Jackson said, "That's what I hope. I can hardly believe it, but I feel there must be twenty-three ... and perhaps more."

"Then what are we waiting for!" the chief said. "Let's go!"

In a few minutes, Dave turned the

antique handle on their drawer and it came off. Then Kathy tried to move the bottom of the front, and it slid off. There was another secret opening!

"Desk 15," said a paper inside. A paper marked POST ROADS was hidden inside the secret opening, too.

Mrs. Jackson said, "This paper looks like a list of all the roads and towns around New York and Boston where mail was carried two hundred years ago." With great care, she put it into a folder.

She said, "I feel as if I'm looking at a treasure chest."

"Me, too," said Bill. "It's like looking for pirate gold."

Then in came an F.B.I. woman with a machine and a screen.

"It's the machine to look at the micro-film strips from the little desk," said Mr. Street.

When the film was in place, everyone gasped. On the screen was page after page of handwriting. The pages told about all the things from Mrs. Morton's house.

Mr. Street turned a knob until he found the pages about the desk.

"I can't believe it!" exclaimed Dave. "There are more than thirty pages about this desk!"

Mrs. Tandy said, "And look there! It has forty-two hiding places.

"And this tells how to open them all!"

Mrs. Jackson said, "Look. It says the desk belonged to Ben Franklin. He had the hiding places made in it. He hid secret papers there in case his house was searched by the British soldiers."

Bill said, "Let's get going on them. I can't wait."

By noon, they had opened 28 hiding places.

They had found all sorts of papers, and 11 more letters. One of them even began, "General Washington, Sir."

"Where do we look next?" asked Bill.

"Right here," said Mr. Street, pointing to two card tables.

An F.B.I. man was putting two big boxes on the tables. Mop ran around one of the tables, trying to get at the boxes.

"What's in those?" asked Mrs. Tandy.

"Books?" asked Kathy.

"Tools?" asked Mrs. Jackson.

"Some detective!" shouted Sammy, sniffing like a hunting dog. "This is MUCH more important!" He looked inside a box, reached in, and sat down with chopsticks in his hand.

Mr. Street laughed. "The citizens of the United States of America are about to give its detectives a lunch of Chinese food."

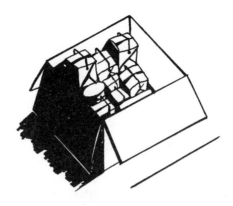

"It tastes great," Sammy said around a mouthful of noodles.

"But how come you brought hot dogs, too?"

Mr. Street said, "Actually, Sammy, it's a very AMERICAN meal.

"Chinese Americans introduced Chinese food to our country. And hot dogs came from Europe.

"Our one country is made of people from many different places. It even says on all our coins, 'E pluribus unum' ... Out of many, one."

"That's true," Mrs. Tandy said. "Some of my family came from Scotland and some from Norway. And one came from Arabia."

Bill said, "My relatives came from Africa, hundreds of years ago. And from Vietnam."

Dave said, "Mine came from England and Sweden and about five other places."

Kathy said, "Mine came from Russia and Israel."

Chief Hemster said, "Mine are from Ireland and Poland and Mexico and Italy."

Mrs. Jackson said, "My father came from England and my mother from China."

"I don't know where mine came from," said Mr. Street. "I'm mostly Native American, and they were here FIRST! Before anyone else."

"Hey! I don't know where mine came from, either," said Sammy.

Chief Hemster said, "Well, WE know where yours came from, Sammy. From Great Detective Land."

Sammy said, "Well let's finish lunch and get back to being detectives!"

Chapter 11:
The Ruts Are Missing

When they were done with lunch, Sammy leaned back and patted his belly. "I feel as full as a water balloon," he said. "I'm ready to start on that desk again."

But just then an F.B.I. agent ran in to talk to Mr. Street.

"We've got trouble, sir," she said.

"What's wrong, Walker?"

She answered, "I've had eight good agents keeping watch outside the Morton house. I even had men on the roof. No one came out of that house. But when we went in to make the arrests, the Ruts were gone!"

Mr. Street said, "WHAT? They MUST be in the house! You and the others are top agents. The Ruts could not just sneak past you."

"Well," said Walker. "The house is full of furniture, but we can't find the Ruts. We've searched top to bottom."

Mr. Street ran to the car. "Come on, everyone. Let's go!"

At the house, they followed the F.B.I. agents inside.

They searched the downstairs first ...

    the antique shop

    the back room

    a bathroom

... and a storage room.

There was no sign of the Ruts.

Then Mr. Street called, "Let's look upstairs." The F.B.I. agents climbed the steps.

Sammy and Bill lifted Dave up the stairs in his chair.

"Hey!" Sammy exclaimed as he looked around. "This is like a museum!"

Mr. Street said, "Walker, you've checked every wardrobe in the house?"

"Yes, sir," she answered. "They are all big enough for a person to hide in. But no luck, sir."

"What's a wardrobe?" Sammy asked.

Kathy answered, "You know, it's a big wooden closet. We read about one in *The*

Lion, The Witch, and the Wardrobe. It's a big wooden piece of furniture. It's for storing things. You put it into a room that doesn't have enough closets."

Bill said, "Come into this room, Sammy. Here are four wardrobes. Look, this one has a place to hang clothes. It has some drawers in it, too."

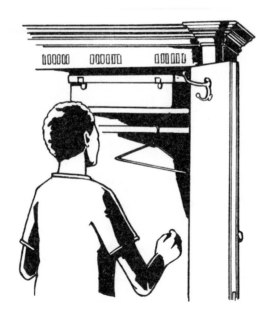

Mr. Street called from the living room, "Let's take a look at the next floor."

On the third floor were two huge bedrooms FILLED with dozens of wardrobes. Wardrobes stood back to back in the middle of the rooms, and wardrobes lined the walls.

The F.B.I. agents looked into each one of them. There were antique clothes in them all, but nobody hiding.

They all walked back to the hall. Mr. Street said, "Well, now you all had a look. Does anyone have any new ideas?"

Dave said, "I've got an idea, sir."

Everyone turned to him.

Mr. Street said, "What's on your mind, Dave?"

Dave began to whisper. "Remember when Kathy was talking about that book? Well, in the book, a child finds a whole secret world ... by walking through the

back of a wardrobe, behind the clothes.
Well, I've got an idea of where the Ruts
are this very minute."

Mrs. Jackson whispered, "Where?"

Dave whispered, "One of these
wardrobes may lead to a secret room. Or
even to a secret tunnel."

Mrs. Jackson said, "You know, that might be the answer!"

Bill whispered, "I hope not a secret tunnel. Then they might have gotten away!"

Mrs. Tandy whispered, "My heavens, Mrs. Jackson, it might take days to find the right wardrobe."

Sammy whispered, "What if they ARE in a secret room in one of the walls? They might be watching and listening to us this very minute."

Sammy's hair stuck straight up!

Mr. Street said, "If Dave is right, there are some things we can do to make the hunt easier. I'll talk to my agents first, and then we will go outside to make plans.

"And if you don't mind, we may need your help. You Woodlanders know how these secret panels work better than anyone here."

He took out his cell phone. "Hello, Walker, I want you to get guards up here; one for every room."

Then he spoke to the Woodlanders and Mrs. Jackson. "As soon as my agents are in place, we will go outside to plan how to catch the Ruts once and for all."

Chapter 12:
The Lizard's Hole

When they got outside, Mr. Street said, "The first thing we can do is move every wardrobe out from the wall."

"I see," Bill said. "If a wardrobe will

move, we can look behind it for a secret door into the wall."

Mr. Street said, "Then we can make an ultrasound check."

Sammy asked, "What's that?"

Dave said, "That's where you can tell how solid something is ... by sending sound waves into it."

Bill said, "And you can use it to tell how wide a space is, too."

Sammy said, "I get it. So we will be able to tell which walls might have secret rooms behind them!"

Mr. Street called to Agent Walker, "Have the lab truck bring in the small ultrasound."

Then he said, "Stay with the agent who runs the ultrasound, Sammy. He will show you how it works."

Bill said, "Sammy the Sound Spy!"

Dave said, "Why don't we get a yardstick? Let's measure across the front of the house and then from the front to the back.

"Then we can measure the room sizes. If they come out too small, we can tell there is extra space somewhere in the walls."

Mr. Street said, "Good idea. Walker, get a yardstick. Dave, you and Kathy take charge of it. Here's a notepad to do the math on."

Then they all went inside once more to the shop space on the first floor.

There was one wardrobe there, but it moved out from the wall easily. There was no secret door behind it.

Sammy and the agent worked the ultrasound around every first-floor room.

"Find anything?" Bill asked.

Sammy answered, "Nothing much, except a hollow spot in a storeroom wall.

"But it's only about as wide as a person, and there is no door into it."

Chief Hemster said, "It might be just an air vent ... but let's keep it in mind."

Dave and Kathy figured out that the first-floor room sizes checked out right.

They all went to the second floor.

"Hey, Mr. Street!" Dave called right away. "There is something wrong with the size of this bedroom."

Kathy called from the bedroom in back of it, "This one is off, too. It is about six feet too short."

Chief Hemster said, "Looks like we've got 'em! Let's move these wardrobes away from the walls!"

They moved them away from the walls. There was no secret door.

So they all rushed to the second bedroom. Mrs. Jackson said, "There MUST be a way in here."

But the wardrobes in the second bedroom moved out easily from the walls. No secret door.

Sammy said, "Boy, I'm going to take an ultrasound reading, Dave. Those walls CAN'T be hollow."

But he found they were.

Mrs. Tandy said, "The third floor HAS to hold a secret way in."

Bill and Sammy grabbed Dave in

115

his chair and hurried upstairs with the others.

Now they were in one of the two big bedrooms with wardrobes covering every wall.

Dave and Kathy measured both bedrooms. Dave said, "How can this be? Both these rooms up here measure the full size."

But Mr. Street said, "One of these wardrobes MUST have a back that opens. It MUST lead to a downstairs secret room somehow.

"Sammy, take an ultrasound reading inside each wardrobe on this wall."

The chief said, "That's a good idea. There are so many, and they are so heavy. We don't want to try to move them all out."

So Sammy went inside of the first one. No luck.

Then the second one. "This back wall is solid, too," he said.

"Look at that!" said Mr. Street. "What's wrong with your dog?"

Mop was sniffing at a wardrobe and hopping around. Then he began to scratch at the floor, and he barked, and sniffed again.

Kathy said, "That's how he acts when he smells something good to eat."

Sammy ran across the room to Mop's wardrobe.

"Hold Mop," he said to Kathy. He climbed inside to test it.

"Hey," he whispered. "There's a space in back of this one, like that space in the storeroom wall downstairs. It's a little wider than a person."

Mr. Street stepped inside and lifted out all the clothes. "It's got to open somehow," he said. "Come on, everyone."

So they all began pushing and tapping inside and out.

Then Dave said, "Hey, how about on top?"

Kathy stood on the arms of his chair to look. She cried, "There's a handle up here!"

She pushed it. There was a click, and the whole back wall of the wardrobe opened.

There was an old ladder, which led down to the floor below.

"COME OUT OF THERE!" shouted Mr. Street. "Jake and Liza Rut, you are under arrest."

There was no answer.

Mr. Street called, "We know you're down there. I'm going to count to three. Start up this ladder or I'm coming down after you."

They heard a little bumping sound ... and some angry voices. And then they heard feet on the iron ladder rungs.

Soon they saw the face of Jake Rut.

And then at last, Liza Rut crawled out.

Mr. Street's agents led them away.

Sammy said, "She didn't have her crocodile smile this time. She looked just like a lizard coming out of its hole."

Chapter 13:
A Letter from Washington

Sammy said, "Wait a minute! If this space behind the wall is a passageway, what about the other ultrasound reading? You know, the one on the first floor."

Mrs. Tandy said, "I think it used to be a passageway too. I bet this house WAS built to hide slaves running to freedom. I think we are standing in a station of the Underground Railroad."

Mr. Street said, "Let's see what's down there. Right now." He ordered flashlights.

Then down they went.

Dave lowered himself on the ladder and the others carried him over to a ...

Bed! "Wow!" Sammy squeaked. "Look at this place!"

They looked down a tunnel-shaped room.

From one end to the other were seven old beds, head to foot, and a bookshelf full of canned food, and an old hand-pump sink.

Kathy said, "Here's what Mop was trying to find."

She held up an open can of tuna. "It

must have been part of the Ruts' lunch."

Sammy ran to the other end of the long, skinny room. "There's a ladder here leading down."

He went down it and called, "It doesn't go anywhere."

Bill said, "Years ago, it must have led to another secret door and to freedom."

Mrs. Tandy was looking at one of the old beds. "What's that under there?" she asked.

On the floor, sticking out just a little from under the bed, were some dried-up-looking papers.

Mr. Street used a hanky to pick up the pages. He laid them in a row on the bed. "Don't touch them," he said. "These may be the papers Mrs. Rut got from the big desk. They may have fingerprints."

Mrs. Jackson leaned over to look at the papers.

"Amazing!" she exclaimed.

"What are they?" the others asked, bending over for a closer look.

"A letter," Mrs. Jackson said. "It is signed by one of Washington's captains. And it has detailed plans for the war in 1776, when we won our freedom from England."

Bill said, "I bet Mrs. Rut was going to sell the letter and have enough money for years."

Mr. Street said, "But now, instead, it will go to a museum, for all Americans to see.

"And all because of Mrs. Morton and Mrs. Jackson and Chief Hemster and the F.B.I and the Woodlanders."

"And Mop!" Sammy said.

Upstairs, Mop heard his name and barked.

■　　■　　■

The next morning, Sunday, the Woodlanders were out in their clubhouse.

Sammy said, "Boy, wasn't it exciting when Chief Hemster opened the last secret hiding place in the desk!"

"Yes," said Mrs. Tandy. "And how about that map of the British army camp? It felt like we were looking back into history."

Just then, they heard the doorbell.

Bill went into the house and came back waving a big, cream-colored letter.

"Listen, everyone," he said. "You're not going to believe this. Here's a letter from Washington, for us!"

"But he's dead," said Sammy.

Bill said, "Not GEORGE Washington! Washington, D.C., the capital. It's from the PRESIDENT!"

Sammy said, "Don't just stand there! Open it! He's probably writing to thank me personally for all my help!"

Bill began to read.

Dear Becky Tandy; Kathy, Bill, and
Sammy Westburg; and David Briggs:

Mr. Street of the F.B.I. has already told me about you.
He wrote of your great help in finding a treasure trove
of historical things for our nation.

I'm writing for all the people of the United States. I am
asking you to be guests in the White House in
Washington, D.C. Please come next Fourth of July to
take part in the celebration.

And don't forget to bring your detective dog!

I hope you will come.

It was signed by the President.

For once, Sammy did not say anything.
His mouth just hung open.

Mrs. Tandy said, "My goodness!"

Then she got up, hurried into the house, and came out with a huge platter of oatmeal cookies and a pitcher of milk.

She said, "These were for after dinner, but NOW is the time for a party. We have to practice for the Fourth of July."

Then Sammy ran into the woods, and came back with five huge leaves.

"Party hats," he said, and he held the biggest leaf onto his own head.

And in a minute, all the Woodlanders were wearing leaf hats, and dancing around with Mop in the morning sun.